"For when people get caught up with that which is right and they are willing to sacrifice for it, there is no stopping point short of victory."

—Dr. Martin Luther King Jr.

MEMPHIS, MART MOUNT

IN, AND THE
AINTOP

THE SANITATION STRIKE OF 1968

Alice Faye Duncan

Illustrated by R. Gregory Christie

CALKINS CREEK
AN IMPRINT OF HIGHLIGHTS
Honesdale, Pennsylvania

This story was mined from history books and the memories of a Memphis teacher. When she was a child, she marched in the Memphis sanitation strike with her mother and father.

Men, women, and children contributed to the strike in 1968. Whole families sacrificed their comforts. They suffered for the cause. However, Dr. Martin Luther King Jr. paid the highest cost. He gave his life to the struggle for freedom and justice.

MEMPHIS—1968

I remember Memphis.

I remember the stinking sanitation strike.

Alley cats, rats, and dogs rummaged through piles of trash.

Black men marched through Memphis with protest signs raised high.

I also marched in '68 with red ribbons in my hair.

I remember Memphis and legions of noblemen.

I remember broken glass and the voice of a fallen King.

Fire, smoke, and ashes ravaged midnight cityscapes.

Black men marched for honor, and I must tell the story.

You must tell the story—so that no one will forget it.

MUD PUDDLES

The conflict started in January—cold and wet with rain. Poor wages for black sanitation workers sparked grumblings of a labor strike. In stormy February, death made the grumblings swell to a loud, blasting rage. I know—I was there as clouds covered the Memphis sky. I had skipped outside to splash and play on the sidewalk in mud puddles.

"Lorraine! Lorraine!"

Mama called my name. I could feel it—a punishment was on the way. But when Daddy ran up the porch distressed and out of breath, Mama ignored my muddy shoes on her clean kitchen floor.

Bad news traveled at lightning speed. There was a tragic accident on a Memphis garbage truck. Two black men working in the rain never made it home for dinner. Their names still live with me. Echol Cole and Robert Walker dumped garbage with my daddy.

Several Memphis garbage trucks were old and unsafe. The trucks were not maintained.

According to my daddy, a packer blade malfunctioned, crushing his friends.

Daddy told Mama, "It ain't right to die like that."

Mama shook her head, and I saw a new storm rising up.

I saw it in their eyes.

MARCHING ORDERS

Memphis sanitation workers shared one common trait. Like my daddy, most of the men were black. They carried rusted garbage barrels as slop dripped down their clothes. White managers called them ugly names, too ugly to repeat.

The average pay for sanitation workers was $1.70 an hour. Daddy called it "starvation pay." Even with a full-time job, he needed government help to buy groceries for our family.

Sanitation workers formed a labor union to advocate their rights. Better pay seemed close at hand. The labor union encouraged better treatment and safety on the job, but the men faced opposition from Memphis mayor Henry Loeb.

Tall like a giant and stubborn like a mule, Mayor Loeb said no to a pay increase. He did not acknowledge the workers' labor union— the American Federation of State, County and Municipal Employees (AFSCME) Local 1733. To insult the men even further, Mayor Loeb gave little assistance to the Cole and Walker families.

When they could take the abuse no more, 1,300 men deserted their garbage barrels. They organized a labor strike on February 12, 1968.

In the morning and afternoon, for sixty-five days, sanitation workers marched fourteen blocks through the streets of downtown Memphis. From Clayborn Temple to the steps of City Hall, they squared their shoulders, raised their heads, and carried their picket signs.

My daddy marched in that number. He marched for better pay. He marched for decent treatment. My daddy marched for me.

WINTER BLUES

The strike crippled garbage collection with terrific success.

Replacement workers operated 38 garbage trucks while a whopping 180 trucks stayed parked at the city barn. Sidewalks turned unsightly by the end of February. Loose paper with crushed cans, empty boxes, and food scraps littered the Memphis streets.

With Daddy on the picket line and less money in the house, he rolled pennies to pay our rent. The phone bill went unpaid. One week we had no lights. And when classmates visited the candy lady on their way home from school, they bought cookies, pickles, and peppermint sticks. I walked home empty-handed.

That year, when I was nine years old, I learned what the grown folks knew. Trouble visits every life. But as strikers marched through sun and rain, help came in many forms.

A group of Memphis preachers formed Community on the Move for Equality (COME). The organization used church donations to help strikers pay their bills.

The National Association for the Advancement of Colored People (NAACP) organized boycotts to support the strike. My mama answered their call. In her right hand she carried her boycott sign. In her left, she held my hand.

Together we marched past downtown stores with shiny storefront windows. Pretty shoes made me smile. But Mama's money stayed in her purse, and I wore old shoes all winter.

TROUBLE

Every night Daddy drove his blue jalopy to jam-packed rallies where strikers sang freedom songs.

We shall overcome,
We shall overcome,
We shall overcome someday!

Music lightened the heavy mood.

Daddy clapped his large black hands. He also listened to Memphis preachers who plotted out strike strategies and delivered fiery speeches to encourage the striking men.

As winter turned into spring, experienced union leaders with AFSCME flew into Memphis from Washington, DC. They spoke with the striking workers as advocates and strategists. Still nothing changed.

The mayor railed *NO!* to every labor request, and my daddy kept right on marching.

One night as I finished homework in the dark by fading candlelight, Mama pleaded, "William . . . maybe you should quit the strike and go on back to work."

Daddy hugged Mama tightly.

"Gladys," he insisted, "we gotta hold on till the end."

Then I heard him promise, "Trouble don't last always."

MARTIN

My daddy was a sanitation worker. My mama was a maid. Neither one of them read very well or finished high school. Lifting garbage and cleaning houses was all the work they could find.

When Mama's boss paid her wages on Friday afternoons, he also put old magazines and newspapers in her carry bag. Mama gave the papers to me. I would read the headlines to both my parents, and we'd follow the strike.

I read the headlines that early March when strike negotiations failed. But as Daddy's soles wore thin on his mountain climb, there came a spark of light. Good news filled the air.

Rev. James Lawson, a COME advisor, called his old friend Martin to Memphis.

The headlines encouraged my parents.

Daddy buzzed around the house, "Dr. King is coming to town!"

Mama told Miss Brooks, our neighbor, "Girl, I can't believe it!"

Dr. Martin Luther King Jr. practiced nonviolent protests. He was a champion for social change who marched for racial equality across Mississippi, Alabama, and Washington, DC. It was his persistent demand for justice that inspired President Lyndon B. Johnson to help abolish segregation and sign the Civil Rights Act of 1964.

Since Martin had conquered giants in the valley of injustice, Reverend Lawson believed his powerful friend could help the striking men. That was my silent prayer as I leaned against my daddy's knee and read the news out loud.

SILVER RIGHTS

I did not plainly comprehend the trouble I saw in 1968. Wisdom came slowly over the mounting years. But when I look back now, I understand.

The Memphis struggle was an economic fight. Better wages and pay were a matter of Silver Rights. Poverty was a Silver War. My daddy and his friends were the working poor.

The men sought better wages to feed their families and buy decent homes—not rundown shanties like our rented house. As public servants, sanitation workers deserved better pay to educate their children and give them a future, bright with hope. This was the message Dr. King preached when he arrived in Memphis on March 18.

He said, "All labor has dignity."

Dr. King's voice was loud and stirring.

I listened with my parents from a crowded church pew as the famous leader drafted a plan to march in Memphis with the striking men.

Dr. King set a date for March 22.

Daddy leaned toward Mama's ear. He said, "We need everybody to march that day."

Mama did not waver.

She assured Daddy, "I'll take off work. You can count on me."

Then Mama patted my hand and said, "We will take Lorraine. She can march with us."

OMEN

Yellow daffodils
Sixteen inches under snow
King canceled his march

BEALE STREET

I followed Dr. King during the nightly news on our black-and-white TV.

As president of the Southern Christian Leadership Conference (SCLC) in Atlanta, Georgia, he cared deeply for America's working poor.

Dr. King set out to abolish poverty in the very same way he had raised his voice to abolish racial segregation. He wanted to strengthen labor laws for all Americans. And to make his dream come true, he planned a massive march in Washington, DC, in the spring of 1968.

Dr. King named this new crusade the "Poor People's Campaign."

As he traveled the nation to promote his plans, Dr. King drew national attention to the Memphis strike. He called it a small conflict that presented a big American problem. From coast to coast and especially in the South, public servants and unskilled laborers like my parents were often underpaid and reduced to poverty.

When the strange snow cleared, Dr. King rescheduled his Memphis protest for March 28.

Mama kept me home from school so I could march that day. We stood together with other mothers and children at the back of the protest line—away from possible danger.

My daddy stood tall at the front of the line with striking workers and clergy like Reverend Lawson and Dr. King. Daddy and his friends also carried picket signs bearing four words: I <u>AM</u> A MAN. With or without a pay increase, they demanded Mayor Loeb's respect.

Six thousand people—blacks, whites, men, women, and children—gathered in downtown Memphis.

Police stood guard with tear gas, billy clubs, and guns.

Fifteen minutes into the march there was a sound of breaking glass.

Looters threw bricks and sticks up and down Beale Street. They shattered storefront windows as strikers and strike supporters scattered their way to safety.

Police sprayed tear gas and beat guilty people. They beat innocent people too. Blood splattered everywhere. It was difficult to see, and I was separated from my mama.

I yelled, "Mama! Where are you?"

Daddy found me on the curb. He scooped me up, and we ran to a nearby church. Mama lost her hat and gloves, but she managed to reach us safely.

It was never proven, but rumors said militant teenagers started the Beale Street riot. As for the Memphis morning paper, it called Dr. King a coward because he ran from the violence and was carted away safely in a stranger's passing car.

The news reports disturbed my father.

He raised his fist and fumed, "Dr. King is a bona fide man!"

Mama rubbed her feet and sighed. "Sometimes bad people mess things up for the good people doing good."

TRUCKS AND TANKS

Mayor Loeb issued a state of emergency in response to the Beale Street riot. He imposed a 7:00 p.m. curfew and called four thousand National Guard soldiers to patrol the Memphis streets in military trucks and tanks.

The presence of soldiers restored the peace. But on the following day, the strike seemed to have no end. Mayor Loeb held firmly to his anti-union position, and workers continued to march. The sight of loaded guns did not send them back to work.

From my bedroom window, I saw soldiers in big green tanks creep slowly up the street. I waved to my friend Jan, who sat in her window too. Nobody played outside that day. Fear locked us in our houses.

DREAMERS

Dreamers don't quit.

When challenges arise, dreamers keep on climbing.

My daddy was a dreamer.

Dr. King was a dreamer too. When the Memphis march turned into a riot, the disappointed leader left the city—but he promised to return. He promised to lead a peaceful march in support of the striking workers. And as Dr. King made new plans to protest, death threats rattled his ears. Somebody wanted to kill his dream of economic freedom for the working poor.

Threats did not stop his mountain climb. On April 3, 1968, Dr. King kissed his wife and children. He left his Atlanta home and boarded a flight to Memphis.

I was there on that stormy night Dr. King returned. Clouds blotted out stars in the Memphis sky. Wind whipped through the bending trees. My daddy beamed with hope when he told Mama, "Dr. King is gonna preach tonight at Mason Temple Church."

In Daddy's blue jalopy, we sputtered through pounding rain. We chugged through bursts of lightning and the shrill of tornado sirens. When we entered the church, a preacher named Abernathy stood at the microphone.

Ralph Abernathy was Dr. King's best friend. On that stormy night, he delivered terrible news—Dr. King was sick and resting in a motel room.

Rain-soaked faces grumbled. My daddy did not drive through sheets of rain for Ralph Abernathy. He came to hear Dr. King.

As the crowd listened to speeches about the strike, I slept in Mama's arms. *KABOOM!* A voice like the evening thunder shook me from my sleep.

It was Dr. King. Like Moses on the mountain, he charged men, women, and children to make the world a promised land flowing with freedom and justice.

Like a man preaching his own funeral, Dr. King used vivid words to paint the story of his life. He described his challenges and triumphs during the civil rights movement. And in the face of death threats, Dr. King spoke boldly. He encouraged Memphis strikers and strike supporters to march, boycott, and raise their voices for worker rights until victory was won.

His voice boomed, "I may not get there with you. But I want you to know tonight, that we, as a people, will get to the promised land."

The crowd rose up with a deafening shout.

My daddy yelled, "Amen!"

My mama yelled, "Praise the Lord!"

An old man hollered, "We can't stop now!"

Dreamers never quit.

LORRAINE

My name is Lorraine like the Memphis motel.

Many years have passed, but the building still stands.

The Lorraine Motel is a storied shrine.

Dr. King shared his last meal and rested there on April 4, 1968.

The leader spent his last hour on the second floor in room 306 where he talked with Ralph Abernathy and Samuel Kyles. They joked and laughed the way good friends do, and they spoke of plans for an evening rally with the striking workers.

The laughter did not last for long.

Evil showed its ugly head as James Earl Ray hunkered down in the open window of a boarding house. Perched seventy yards from the Lorraine Motel, the escaped convict pointed his rifle at room 306 and waited.

He saw his target at one minute past six.

Dr. King stepped on the balcony where he greeted friends in the parking lot.

Ray fired his gun, and a bullet pierced the dreamer's neck.

News of Dr. King's assassination spread quickly. In Washington, DC, Chicago, and Baltimore, young people expressed their grief with looting and raging fires.

Mayor Henry Loeb called for the return of the National Guard. There was not much looting in Memphis. But a fire burned in me as I

stretched across my bed and listened to radio station WDIA. Between finger-snapping hits by Aretha Franklin and James Brown, the black disc jockey cried for the loss of Dr. King.

I cried too when Dr. King was shot. I also wrote a poem in my school notebook. Writing served me better than breaking glass. And Mama posted my poem on the crumbling wall of our rented house.

THE KING IS DEAD
by Lorraine Jackson

Not long ago,
There lived a King.
He did not sleep in a castle.
He did not wear a crown.
He did not rule a royal court
Or ride in chariots.

The King marched in the streets.
He lived to help the poor.
He lived for peace and love.
Hate killed the King.
The King is dead.
What will the people do?

BLACK WIDOW

Coretta Scott King flew to Memphis committed to a plan.

Dr. King had pledged to support the sanitation strike with a nonviolent march. Despite her broken heart, Mrs. King and members of SCLC helped to keep her husband's pledge on April 8, 1968.

The memorial march served as a tribute to honor Dr. King's life. It also reminded Mayor Loeb that workers would strike and continue their upward climb until justice was received.

In a wave of forty thousand people, I marched that day between my mama and daddy. Those who marched with us were ministers, labor leaders, political figures, entertainers, and everyday people from Memphis and around the nation.

Nobody spoke a word. We raised our protest signs.

Honor King: End Racism!

Union Justice Now!

Mrs. King marched from Memphis. Behind a veil of mourning, she buried her love in Georgia.

VICTORY ON A BLUE NOTE

The Memphis Sanitation Strike ended on April 16, 1968.

Mayor Loeb never bargained with the workers. President Lyndon B. Johnson sent James Reynolds, a top US labor official, to negotiate a settlement.

Reynolds brokered an agreement between the sanitation workers and the Memphis City Council. In the final deal, the city of Memphis recognized the workers' labor union, the men received a pay increase of fifteen cents an hour, and they were promised job promotions based on merit—not race.

I remember that glad day the stinking strike came to an end. It was the Tuesday after Easter. Daddy marched proudly into the house and smiled at Mama and me. He picked me up, kissed my face, and cried in Mama's neck. Mama squeezed us tightly as tears filled her eyes.

So much was won.

So much was lost.

Freedom is never free.

MOUNTAINTOP

Dream big.
Walk tall.
Be strong.
March on.
Don't quit.
Never stop.
Climb up the MOUNTAINTOP!

MEMPHIS SANITATION STRIKE—1968 TIMELINE*

January 1 — Henry Loeb is sworn into office as the new Memphis mayor.

February 1 — Two black sanitation workers are killed in an accident on a malfunctioning garbage truck.

February 12 — Memphis sanitation employees strike after failed attempts to resolve work grievances. Only 38 of 180 garbage trucks move from the city barn.

February 13 — An international union official visits from Washington, DC, to meet with Mayor Loeb. He calls for union recognition of the American Federation of State, County and Municipal Employees (AFSCME) Local 1733 and negotiations to resolve their labor grievances. Mayor Loeb vows to hire new men if strikers don't report to work.

February 14 — Mayor Loeb orders a back-to-work ultimatum for February 15. City police escort the few garbage trucks in operation. Negotiations between the city and labor union fail. Ten thousand tons of garbage litter the Memphis streets.

February 16 — Union leaders ask the Memphis City Council to help them in their labor struggle. However, council members support Mayor Loeb. The Memphis chapter of the National Association for the Advancement of Colored People (NAACP) endorses the sanitation strike.

February 18 — AFSCME International president Jerry Wurf arrives in Memphis. He states that the strike will end when worker demands are met. Memphis ministers call a meeting with Mayor Loeb and union leaders. It is moderated by a Memphis rabbi. The meeting fails.

February 20 — In support of the strike, the NAACP organizes a citywide boycott of downtown merchants and department stores.

February 22 — In a meeting with one thousand striking workers, black City Councilman Fred Davis urges the city of Memphis to recognize the labor union. This meeting ends without action.

February 23 — Memphis police attack strikers with mace during a march on Main Street.

February 24 — Black Memphis ministers form Community on the Move for Equality (COME), a citywide organization to support the strike and the local boycotts.

*Based on the AFSCME timeline: AFSCME Local 1733, Memphis, Tennessee

February 25 — Memphis ministers ask their church congregations to boycott and participate in local marches to support the strike.

February 26 — Daily marches from Clayborn Temple to City Hall begin.

February 27 — Mayor Loeb refuses to compromise, and hundreds demonstrate at City Hall.

February 29 — Mayor Loeb mails each striking worker an invitation to return to work without union recognition.

March 1 — Mayor Loeb blames strikers for the broken windows and recent vandalism at his home.

March 3 — Gospel singers hold a singing marathon at Mason Temple Church to raise money for strikers and demonstrate community support.

March 4 — A Tennessee senator proposes a bill to create a state mediation board to resolve the strike impasse. Mayor Loeb opposes the bill.

March 5 — Rev. James Lawson announces Dr. Martin Luther King Jr. will visit Memphis to organize a mass march with thousands of strike supporters.

March 6 — Strikers stage a mock funeral at City Hall to mourn the death of freedom in Memphis.

March 8 — Strike supporters are blamed for trash fires throughout South Memphis neighborhoods.

March 9 — The National Guard conducts riot drills at the mayor's request.

March 11 — Black Memphis teenagers skip school to participate in a strike protest.

March 14 — Roy Wilkins, national leader of the NAACP, visits Memphis to support the labor strike.

March 18 — Dr. King speaks at Mason Temple in Memphis. More than 17,000 people gather to hear him. He calls for a citywide protest on March 22.

March 22 — A record snowstorm of sixteen inches cancels the march.

March 28 — The rescheduled protest erupts into a riot on Beale Street with Dr. King leading the march. Police attack crowds with tear gas and nightsticks. Teenager Larry Payne is shot to death by an officer. Four thousand National Guardsmen move into the city with army tanks, and a curfew is set for 7:00 p.m.

March 29 — Dr. King leaves Memphis but makes a promise to return for a peaceful protest. Escorted by National Guard soldiers, more than three hundred sanitation workers and ministers march silently from Clayborn Temple to City Hall. President Johnson offers assistance to resolve the strike. Mayor Loeb rejects his offer.

March 31 — Dr. King cancels a trip to Africa and plans his Memphis return to lead a peaceful march.

April 1 — Memphis curfew ends.

April 2 — The National Guard is withdrawn from the city as hundreds of Memphians attend Larry Payne's funeral.

April 3 — Dr. King returns to Memphis on a stormy night to address a rally at Mason Temple and deliver his "I've Been to the Mountaintop" speech. It will be his very last sermon.

April 4 — James Earl Ray assassinates Dr. King on the balcony outside room 306 at the Lorraine Motel.

April 5 — More than one hundred cities across the nation experience looting and fires in the aftermath of Dr. King's death. The Federal Bureau of Investigation (FBI) begins an international search for James Earl Ray, while President Johnson sends US labor official James Reynolds to settle the garbage strike in Memphis.

April 6 — Reynolds meets separately with Mayor Loeb and the striking men over the course of ten days. The two groups never gather in the same room.

April 8 — Mrs. Coretta Scott King and forty thousand supporters lead a silent memorial march through downtown Memphis as a tribute to her husband and in support of the striking men.

April 9 — Dr. King's funeral is held in Atlanta, Georgia.

April 10 — Without publicity or attention from the media, James Reynolds continues labor meetings with city leaders and union officials.

April 16 — AFSCME union leaders for Local 1733 announce that an agreement has been reached. The striking workers vote to accept the deal, and the strike ends.

MUSEUM TO VISIT

National Civil Rights Museum at the Lorraine Motel

450 Mulberry Street
Memphis, Tennessee
civilrightsmuseum.org

The National Civil Rights Museum, established in 1991, is located at the site where Dr. Martin Luther King Jr. was assassinated in 1968. The Memphis museum—a Smithsonian affiliate—chronicles the history of the American civil rights movement and examines global human rights issues in the twenty-first century. Exhibits and lectures at the museum serve as catalysts for social justice.

SOURCES

"1968 AFSCME Memphis Sanitation Workers' Strike Chronology." AFSCME. afscme.org/union/history/mlk/1968-afscme-memphis-sanitation-workers-strike-chronology.

Bausum, Ann. *Marching to the Mountaintop: How Poverty, Labor Fights, and Civil Rights Set the Stage for Martin Luther King, Jr.'s Final Hours*. Washington, DC: National Geographic Children's Books, 2012.

Beifuss, Joan. *At the River I Stand: Memphis, the 1968 Strike, and Martin Luther King*. Memphis, TN: B & W Books, 1985.

Honey, Michael. *Going Down Jericho Road: The Memphis Strike, Martin Luther King's Last Campaign*. New York: Norton, 2007.

Jackson, Hattie Elie. *65 Dark Days in '68: Reflections: Memphis Sanitation Strike*. Southaven, MS: King's Press, 2004.

King, Martin Luther, Jr., and Cornel West. *The Radical King*. Boston: Beacon Press, 2014.

McMillin, Zack. "Moving Mountains: Martin Luther King Jr. Forty Years Later." *Memphis (TN) Commercial Appeal,* February 17, 2008, sec. V1–V10.

Sides, Hampton. *Hellhound on His Trail: The Stalking of Martin Luther King, Jr. and the International Hunt for His Assassin*. New York: Doubleday, 2010.

Starks-Umoja, Almella. Telephone interview with author, June 29, 2015.

_____. Telephone interview with author, July 6, 2015.

SOURCE NOTES

ACKNOWLEDGMENTS

I owe abounding gratitude to Dr. Almella Starks-Umoja. She was kind to share her memories of the strike with me. In 1968, her father, Rev. Henry Logan Starks, was pastor of Saint James A.M.E. Church in Memphis, Tennessee. Reverend Starks was also a community organizer and strategist for the sanitation strike. Almella marched with both of her parents during strike protests. She also heard Dr. Martin Luther King Jr. deliver his "I've Been to the Mountaintop" speech at Mason Temple Church. As an eyewitness to these historical events, she was generous to read my manuscript in its many iterations and forms. There are no adequate words to express my appreciation for her help. Thank you!

In memory of Rev. Henry Logan Starks
        —AFD

For Gabriella Christie
        —RGC

Text copyright © 2018 by Alice Faye Duncan
Illustrations copyright © 2018 by R. Gregory Christie

Calkins Creek
An Imprint of Highlights
815 Church Street
Honesdale, Pennsylvania 18431
calkinscreekbooks.com
Printed in China

ISBN: 978-1-62979-718-2

Library of Congress Control Number: 2017949844

First edition
10 9 8 7 6 5 4 3 2 1

Design by Barbara Grzeslo
The text is set in Frutiger.
The artwork is painted with Acryla Gouache.